Papa's Stories

written and illustrated by Dolores Johnson

Macmillan Publishing Company   New York

Maxwell Macmillan Canada   Toronto

Maxwell Macmillan International   New York   Oxford   Singapore   Sydney

To my editor, Judith R. Whipple

The text of this book is set in 14 pt. ITC Garamond Light. The illustrations are rendered in watercolor
and colored pencil on paper.
1 3 5 7 9 10 8 6 4 2

Library of Congress Cataloging-in-Publication Data
Johnson, Dolores.
Papa's stories / written and illustrated by Dolores Johnson. — 1st ed.   p.   cm.
Summary: Kari loves to have her father read to her, until she
discovers that he cannot read and is making the stories up.
ISBN 0-02-747847-5
[1. Literacy—Fiction.   2. Fathers and daughters—Fiction.]
I. Title.
PZ7.J631635Pap   1994   [E]—dc20   93-17534

When Kari was just a little girl, she waited every day by the front door for her father to come home. And when Papa strode into the house, his long legs covered in dirty blue jeans, he asked, "Where's my little princess?"

While Mama cooked supper and Papa bathed a day's worth of soil from his skin, Kari chose a book filled with words and colorful pictures. Papa settled into his favorite chair, his skin smelling as fresh as fir trees. Kari climbed into his lap and snuggled into the crook of his arm. Then Papa read her a story.

Kari's father read that day, as he often did, from a big red book that was Kari's favorite. "This is the story of Little Miss Too-Big-for-Her-Red-Britches," he began. "Her mama told her, 'Daughter, it's 'bout time you got out of the house for a spell and had yourself a picnic. Take your shoes off and cool your toes by the side of a bubblin' spring. Shade your face from the sun under an ole oak tree. But whatever you do, don't share a crumb of your food with that crooked Eustace W. Evilfella.'"

"Who's Eusta…Eustace…who's that, Papa?"
"Here he is. He's this mean ole hairy wolf."

"And take care
on your way to
Grandma's house,"
said her mother,
as she waved
goodbye.

There were times Kari and Papa got so wrapped up in their reading that Mama would have to call them again and again to supper. And then there were times Mama let supper sit while she joined Kari and Papa on the porch in the moonlight. Or, during winter's chilliest evenings, the whole family would snuggle up close together on the sofa and read books by the light of the fire.

Papa read stories about strange little boys who swallowed
magic till they were full of beans, and giants who were angry
because their mustaches didn't fit.

He read about stingy hags who didn't want to share their apples, and little girls with seven brothers the size of toadstools.

He read books about girls who traveled by pumpkin-wagon, and old biddies with corns on their toes. Kari loved to hear her father read the stories.

When Papa couldn't finish the books before supper, he finished them as he put Kari to bed. Most likely, the story had changed a bit and usually got more interesting. One time when he read again from Kari's favorite book, Little Miss Too-Big-for-Her-Red-Britches wasn't going on a picnic anymore. She was going to visit her grandmama, who had grown whiskers so fierce no one wanted to kiss her. Another time the story about the bean-eating boy had changed. Now he was climbing the beanstalk to be first in line to heaven. "I love the way the stories change every time you read them, Papa."

As Kari grew older, Papa said, "You're getting so big, little princess. Soon I'll be sittin' in your lap instead of you sittin' in mine."

"Oh, Papa," giggled Kari. "I'll never be that big."

"No, but you are growin' up," he said. "You've almost finished kindergarten. You've got new friends. Soon things may change between you and your papa."

Kari told him, "Things will never change, 'cause you're the best papa a girl could ever have. I'll always love you, no matter what."

One day Kari brought home an older neighbor girl named Jennifer. They played dress-up, some games, and they played with Kari's dolls. Then Jennifer picked up Kari's favorite big red book and said, "Oh, I love this book, *Little Red Riding Hood*."

"No," said Kari. "That book is the story of Little Miss Too-Big-for-Her-Red-Britches. I know, 'cause my papa must've read it to me a half a million times." Kari opened the book and turned the pages. "See. This is where her grandmama grew those terrible whiskers."

"No, let me show you. This is 'Little…Red…Riding…Hood,'" said Jennifer as she pointed out the words on the cover. She took the book out of Kari's hands and pointed out every word as she read the story from the beginning. "'Once there was a little girl who lived near the woods. She wore a cape with a red riding hood….'"

That evening, while Kari's mother cooked supper in the kitchen, Kari asked her questions that had been bothering her all afternoon. "Do words change every time you read them, Mama?"

Kari's mother stopped stirring. "They shouldn't, baby," she said. "Written words are always the same."

"If a person can't read, does that make them dumb?"

Kari's mother turned to face her. "No, darling. Most of the time it means they just haven't had a chance to learn."

"If someone tells you one thing for a long, long time, and you find out it's another, could they be lying about how much they love you, too?" Kari asked.

Kari's mother put her arms around her daughter. "Your father loves you so very much. But you're right. There should be no secrets between children and their parents. I think you and your papa really need to talk," she said.

So Kari waited by the window for her father to come home. And when he tried to pick her up Kari asked him, "Can't you really read, Papa? Were you ever gonna tell me?"

Papa slowly let Kari down. Then he sat in his favorite chair and pulled Kari to him. Papa stumbled around with words that seemed really hard to say. "I never, ever intended to fool you, little princess. It was so special to me the way you loved to hear my stories. I just couldn't find a way to tell you I didn't know how to read."

"Why didn't you ever learn, Papa?"

"When I was young, I didn't care enough about learnin'. And there was no one who seemed to care about me. When I got older, I didn't love myself enough to even try."

Kari told her father, "Well, I love you so much. I love you and Mama so much. So as soon as I learn to read in school, I'm gonna teach you."

Papa held out his arms, and father and daughter embraced. But then Papa picked up Kari's favorite book and began very, very slowly: "'Once there was a little girl who lived near the woods. She wore a cape with a red riding hood.'"

"Papa! You *can* read!"

"I realized a while ago it was time for me to do better. I decided that I had a real good reason in my life to make a special effort to learn again. So I asked your mother to teach me how to read."

Kari snuggled even tighter in her father's arms as he continued to read *Little Red Riding Hood*. Then she stopped him right in the middle of a word. "Excuse me, Papa. When you finish this book, read it to me again like you always did. I love the extra-special way you read the stories."